KT-116-415

Easy words to read

Frog on a log

Phil Roxbee Cox

Illustrated by Stephen Cartwright

Edited by Jenny Tyler

Language consultant:

Marlynne Grant

BSc, CertEd, MEdPsych, PhD, AFBPs, CPsychol

HIGHLAND
LIBRARIES

0107/046

There is a yellow duck to find on every page.

First published in 2001 by Usborne Publishing Ltd. Usborne House, 83-85 Saffron Hill, London EC1N 8RT, England. www.usborne.com
Copyright ©2001 Usborne Publishing Ltd.

The name Usborne and the device ⊕ ♀ are Trade Marks of Usborne Publishing Ltd. All rights reserved. No part of this publication may be reproduced, stored in a retrieval system, or transmitted in any form or by any means electronic, mechanical, photocopying, recording or otherwise, without prior permission of the publisher. UE. Printed in Hong Kong, China. First published in America in 2001

Frog sits on his log
by the bog.

With one big hop,
he jumps over
the bog.

3

Off he goes! Frog likes to jog.

"I'm a jogging frog
from the log
by the bog."

5

Frog's jogging has ended.
It is foggy.

Out of the fog
runs Pup the dog.

Pup can't see.

He bumps into Frog's log.

Frog is back up on his log. Along trots Big Pig in the fog.

Pig is looking for
Pup the dog.

Now he bumps into Frog's log...

Next day, it is sunny.

"Bump into my log!" says Frog.

Is Frog trying to be funny?

"Bump your log!"
barks Pup the dog.

"You will not call us silly dog and hog?"

"No, bump away!" croaks grinning Frog.
"I cannot fall off. I'm strapped to my log."

So Big Pig and Pup the dog
bump into the log...

...which tips back into the bog...

...taking with it foolish Frog. 15

Frog is agog.

"Now it is me who is silly. A silly frog!"